All

Their Names

Were Courage

All Their Names Were Courage

A Novel of the Civil War

∽ ❧ ∾

SHARON

PHILLIPS

DENSLOW

∽ ❧ ∾

Greenwillow Books
An Imprint of HarperCollins Publishers

*With special thanks to the reference librarians
at the Farquier County Library, for helping find
Tom Telegraph's name; to Deb Root Shell at the Western Reserve
Historical Society Library; to Dr. Tom Mahl and Andrew Keyser,
for fact-checking the manuscript; and to my friends,
who cheered me on as I worked on this story and have been
patiently waiting for me to finish it.*

For information address HarperCollins Children's Books, a division of
HarperCollins Publishers, 1350 Avenue of the Americas, New York,
NY 10019. www.harperchildrens.com

The text of this book is set in Cochin and Kennerly.
Book design by Chad W. Beckerman.

Library of Congress Cataloging-in-Publication Data
Denslow, Sharon Phillips.

All their names were Courage / by Sharon Phillips Denslow.
p. cm.
"Greenwillow Books."
Summary: In 1862, as William Burd fights in the Civil War,
he exchanges letters with his sister, Sallie, who is also
writing to Confederate and Union generals asking about
their horses in order to write a book.
ISBN 0-06-623810-2 (trade). ISBN 0-06-623809-9 (lib. bdg.) 1. United
States—History—Civil War, 1861–1865—Juvenile fiction. [1. United
States—History—Civil War, 1861–1865—Fiction. 2. War horses—
Fiction. 3. Horses—Fiction. 4. Soldiers—Fiction. 5. Brothers and
sisters—Fiction. 6. Letters—Fiction.] I. Title.
PZ7.D433 Al 2003 [Fic]—dc21 2002035327
1 2 3 4 5 6 7 8 9 10
First Edition

 GREENWILLOW BOOKS

To the horses and riders—

and to Tony, Erin, Kate, Tammy,

Mama, and Daddy, horse enthusiasts all.

And to the memory of my great-grandmother

Sallie McAlister Burd Phillips, who told

her sons the story of the guerrilla soldiers

and her gray mare.

Ajax. Aldebaron. Al
Baldy. Bayard. Billy
Butler. Brigand. Chan
Comanche. Dick T
Daniel Webster. Dec
ater. Gaunt Sorrel.
Hero Highfly. Jack.
Kentuck. King Philip.
he Valley. Lookout. D
Lexington. Little Rebe
Monmouth. Moscow
Richmond. Rifle. Rom
he East. Sovereign.
Telegraph. Traveller.

A Note to Readers

During the Civil War there were both Union and Confederate supporters in Kentucky. Neighbors and even families often sympathized with different sides. Although Kentucky was a slave state, it never seceded and was not considered in rebellion against the United States government. Dubbed a border state, Kentucky was a gateway to the Deep South. Both Yankee forces and Rebel fighters vied for control of its rivers and forts. No major battles were fought on Kentucky soil, but skirmishes, sabotage, and guerrilla raids swept across the state under some of the most colorful leaders of the war.

⁓ ⌢

July 20, 1862

Dear William,

We had a scare here last week. Some soldiers came riding through—Confederates, others told us. Mama and I weren't close enough to see because when we heard them coming we ran and hid in the cornfield. Charlie refused to follow us and stayed to guard the house. We could hear him barking and the men yelling, then some shots and Charlie was quiet. They shot him almost in the heart, but he lived and is begin-ning to eat again, Mama's corn bread mixed with beans and milk. He can get off the porch now on his own. For a few days he lay on a rag rug by the back door. The soldiers broke many of our dishes and stole most of our food including our last ham. They tore down the back door and the door to the chicken house looking for eggs, and they took three fat pullets. Luckily Daisy was in the back field with her calf and they missed her. Papa was with Roy and Bob cutting hay in the bottoms when the soldiers were here. He heard them and came riding up on Bob like he was a racehorse. We thought he was a leftover soldier until he called our names. He cried when he found us in the field. I didn't cry until I saw the gate open.

William, they stole Belle. I could not sleep for two nights worrying about telling you and then your letter came telling us about Foster getting shot and I felt so bad that your stallion and mare were both gone, but I am glad that Foster saved you because if he had not been there to stop the bullet it would have struck you. Papa says we are all alive and thank God for that. I still have cuts on my face where the corn blades cut me as we ran to hide, but they are getting better. Mama cut her eye but it is nearly well now too.

Yesterday we were picking beans, the ones the soldiers didn't trample, and I was thinking of how much you like fresh beans and biscuits and I couldn't remember what you looked like. I was more scared than when the soldiers came. I ran upstairs and got my picture of you and I carry it around in my pocket now. Do you still have my picture? I hope so. I don't want you to forget what I look like. Please do not get hurt or worse.

Sallie

July 22, 1862

William!! Belle is back. We were finishing supper yesterday when Mama said I hear a horse. We all sat real quiet and we heard it too. Hoofbeats and finally a whicker and I yelled Belle and knocked my chair over and ran to the yard and Belle came running up the path. She looked black instead of gray, her hide was so wet with sweat. And her eyes were wild and she had foam at the corners of her mouth and in her nostrils, but as soon as Papa opened the pasture gate she made for the pond and rolled in the mud and stood in the pond and had a long drink. She spent the rest of the evening grazing, and this morning I gave her a handful of sweet feed Isaac brought over and I curried off all of the dried mud and sweat and Belle acts as if nothing happened. Papa says she was too heavy with foal to keep up with the soldiers so they cut her loose and good Belle came home. Now we have Foster's foal to watch for, which makes it some easier that he was killed.

Your loving sister Sallie

August 12, 1862

Dear Sallie,

Your letters have just arrived. Be glad only food was taken from our home and a few dishes broken. I have witnessed worse. Hoorah for Belle. By now she has foaled. I hope it is a filly. It is a good thing I guess that Belle always has insisted on foaling in summer instead of spring or the soldiers would have gotten a good mare. Charlie will be fine. He is a big strong dog and a brave one too. Maybe we should change his name to Fighting Charlie.

I have poison ivy rash on both hands and arms and on my face. It itches me something fierce, but I cannot complain overmuch as my good friend Tom Banks has a deep gash on his cheek and chin that will not heal properly. We are two swollen-faced soldiers for sure.

Tom is from near Pilot Oak, close to the Tennessee border. He rides a fine red roan he calls Fever. Fever has almost white flanks which present a good target in maneuvers, so Tom spreads mud or tobacco juice to darken them. Tom's uncle was a blacksmith when he was younger. Tom has been giving me some ideas for the smithy Papa and I want to have after the war.

I have a new horse. He is a bay with some walker blood so he rides smooth, but he is stubborn and fights me for the bit. General Grant has been riding the big horse that he found on the battlefield. It is not a bad horse now, but it was pitiful when he took it in. We are marching south tomorrow so must go to bed now. A slight rain has begun. Maybe it will cool things down. I look at your picture every day. I am attaching this to Mama and Papa's letter as paper is scarce. Eat some biscuits and pear preserves for me.

Your brother William

August 20, 1862

Dear William,

Belle has foaled. A colt not a filly, but he is a beauty. He is so woolly you would think he'd been a January foal. His hair is long and pale gray, but around his eyes and nose and legs he is very dark so that he looks as if he has rings around his eyes and is comical-looking. Papa says when he loses his baby fuzz he will be as dark as Foster was. His front hooves have pale stripes in them, which Papa is displeased with since he says pale hooves are not as strong as dark ones. Mama says that is an old wives' tale. Who is right? I have named him Peaceable because he is so gentle and follows us around when we go in the field and hangs by the fence when we are by the house, wanting us to scratch between his ears or rub his nose. I wish you could see him.

Isaac has drawn a picture of him and Belle for you but it is so good we are afraid to send it to you as it could be ruined. Isaac has also drawn a picture of Foster. It looks just like him. I went to town with Isaac and Mr. and Mrs. Mills and Isaac showed his picture of Foster to Mr. Heath, who runs the paper now and is a first cousin to Isaac's mother. He was so impressed he gave Isaac some paper and said he would get some paints for him. This all gave me and Isaac an idea. We want to make a book of warhorses. Isaac could do the pictures and I would write to generals of the war and ask them to tell me some-

thing about their horses. Mr. Mills says Isaac
has too much work to do with Frederick and
James away fighting but Isaac says he will stay
up at night to draw. Mrs. Mills told Mama that
she thought it would help take Isaac's mind off
of worrying about his two brothers, which is
what Papa says about me and you. Papa has
even made us a front and back cover for our book
out of two old oak barn shingles. He sanded
them very thin and they have a beautiful color.
He put two holes in them and gave us some
rawhide to hold the pages in. Mama doesn't care
that I make the book but she says the generals
are too busy with the war to write me back and
that I am wasting my time. What do you think,
William? Would anyone answer me? It would be
a very pretty book with Papa's cover and Isaac's
pictures. And when you come home you could
see it and we would have Foster in it and Belle
with her story of being captured.

I am taking good care of Peaceable and Belle. Charlie still moves a little stiffly but he gets around okay. He has not barked since the soldiers were here. I wonder if he can anymore. Our peaches were so small this year that we just peeled them and ate them, except for two pies Mama made and then it took an apron full for each pie. Are there any peaches where you are? Mama says ours were little because they were pining for you since you could always eat more of them than anyone else without even once getting sick. I tell Peaceable about you so you won't be a stranger to him when you come home.

With love from Sallie

September 1862

Dear Sallie,

How I would love to see Peaceable. It sounds as if he has more of Belle's personality than Foster's, but that will make him a better horse for the family. Several of the men here agree with Father about the pale hooves, but Tom says he had a gray horse with pale hooves that could outrun every horse he ever saw and was never tender-footed or lame. Since neither Foster nor Belle have ever had any trouble with their feet I think Peaceable will turn out okay. I did have a peach this summer, but it was wormy and mealy except for one spot, and that bite was heaven. I don't know if every general would answer you but what can it hurt to try? If any of them are like Grant they are great admirers of horses and perhaps it would give them respite from heavier correspondence to write you back. Everyone writes home and thinks of home to keep from going mad. Generals are probably no different. I have a friend who helps shoe the horses here and he mentioned your horse book to one of Grant's adjutants. I don't know if anything will come of it, but Grant is always surprising us with what he does and doesn't do, so the first correspondence you receive may be from the general himself. That would hush Mama up. We have had a few days of bivouac but I think we have hard business ahead. Tell Isaac to keep drawing those horses. I miss you all.

William

September 7, 1862

Dear William,

Can you smell the tobacco where you are? We have cut it and hung it and it is firing now. I can see small puffs of smoke every once in a while from the barn when the wind quits for a breath. Papa says it is a good harvest. Grandpap rubs the leaves between his thumb and fingers and says it is not as good as the crop of fifty-nine. I can tell he is satisfied though by the way he slaps all the men on the back and grins at the women. We had all the neighbors here yesterday and today working in the fields and barn. I am tired of cooking and washing up. I would rather be with the men bringing in the tobacco. Mr. Mills said that you would not even know a war is going on everyone was so merry. Of course after he said that it was quiet for a long time because we knew we had no right to be in good spirits putting up the tobacco while you and Fred and James and all the other boys are in fields getting shot at. Our barn is the finest tobacco barn of all. I am glad Great-Grandpap built it here so that it is near us, but it does make bringing the tobacco from Grandpap's and Uncle Tobe's a bigger job. Remember when I was scared of the firing room? When I stepped down into it last week with Mama this time it felt safe and peaceful not scary. Not one bit of light found a chink between the wood. And although I do not plan to ever take up snuff or smoking, there is no smell sweeter or richer than an old barn. Tonight the barn itself is puffing away curing the long leaves. I imagine for miles and miles folks can smell our barn.

I miss you William. After all the company our house tonight seems lonely. It is the first tobacco firing I have ever known without you. Mama sniffed my head and said tomorrow we will wash our hair and get the smoke smell out. I think we could wait a day or two longer. I hope you have not taken up any bad army habits like chewing tobacco. Smelling the barn is one thing, having streams of brown tobacco juice running out the sides of your mouth is another.

Love, Sallie

P.S. Mama read over my letter and smiled at the part about your chewing tobacco. She thinks you are too good to ever try it. But I don't know about that. I am composing a letter for the generals. I will send you a copy.

October 1, 1862

Dear Sallie,

It is good to hear you had a good tobacco harvest. I wish I could have been there. It is one of my favorite times as well. We have passed some tobacco barns here in Tennessee, but none of them were working barns so the only tobacco smell for us is around the fires in camp when everyone rolls thin smokers. Some fellows have rounded up some bought rolled ones and when someone offers me one I cannot refuse as it would insult them. But it is not a taste I am fond of yet. The time or two I tried chewing it did not sit well with my intestines. So you should not worry about those bad habits. Speaking of tobacco, a John Embree who recently joined our company entertained us one night by telling us about a wild bay stallion they once had who would eat everything. One day he got loose in the tobacco field and ate his fill. The leaves were young and tender and they didn't kill him. But he foamed brown spit out of his mouth for a day or two. After that he would not touch any feed or hay or anything until he saw another horse or one of the cows tucking in.

He learned his lesson, I guess. John told the story better than I write it.

Your brother William

November 4, 1862

Dear William,

I have copied and mailed eight letters to generals. It was a big undertaking. Mama said I could ruin my eyes writing so much. I am enclosing you a copy of the letter as well as a list of the generals. Mr. Heath helped with addresses. I know it will be a wait for them to even reach the generals and that we will be lucky to hear from any of them. Do you think I should send General Grant a letter even though your friend the blacksmith passed him word about our horse book? I think I will because he may have become busy and forgotten. The first horse Isaac wants to draw is Lee's Traveller, so I hope General Lee will answer. Traveller is a lovely name for a horse. What horses do you and your friends know about that I should include in my list of names?

I guess you know Mama is working for Mr. Heath one day a week setting type while Mrs. Heath is visiting her sister. Peaceable is almost as tall as Belle now, but his legs are so long he still looks like a foal. Papa says he will be taller than Foster. We are halter breaking him now. He is calm about it but he looks puzzled over what we want him to do. I found a horseshoe in the woods the other day. We think it is from one of the soldiers who were here. I'm keeping it to show you. As you can see I'm out of room to write more.

Love, Sallie

Dear Sir,

My friend Isaac Mills and myself, Sarah

McAlister Burd, both eleven and one half years, of Brewers Mill, Kentucky, are writing to generals with regard to your fine horses. We mean to make a book of the horses with pictures drawn by Isaac and letters from generals, such as yourself, telling us some about your favorite horse. We feel that the courageous warhorses and their stories and daring should not be lost. If you have time to correspond back we would be obliged if you could describe your horse in size and configuration, as well as temperament.

We at this time have two horses of our own to include, one being Belle our mare who was captured by marauding soldiers but escaped and returned, and the second being my brother's stallion Foster who was killed in battle. They are not generals' horses but they have been a part of this war in their own way. The soldiers mentioned before also shot our dog but he is mending. I sincerely hope that I have not unduly taken up your time.

Your correspondent,
Sarah Burd (Sallie)
Brewers Mill
Kentucky

The generals I have written so far:

Lee — Confederate
McClellan — Union
Hancock — U
Jackson — C
Hampton — C
Stuart — C
McDowell — U
Thomas — U

I have several other names to write:

    Grant — U
    Meade — U
    Burnside — U
    Joe Johnston — C
    Sheridan — U
    Morgan — C
    Forrest — C
    Ingalls — U
    Pleasonton — U
    R. Taylor — C
    Beauregard — C
    Bragg — C
    Longstreet — C

I don't know if I will write to all of them. It took me some time to finish the eight I mailed. But this is my list I am working from. Who do you think will be the first to answer?

November 30, 1862

Dear William,

I am writing this at the table at Grandmother and Grandpap's. Grandpap is asleep in his chair by the fireplace. His head is hanging so low all I can see is the top of his head. Every so often he snores like a scolding squirrel. Grandmother is mending the hole I tore in my skirt this afternoon. We are trying to be quiet so we don't wake him up. It has been one of those days when he fusses and argues over everything. It started when that Mr. Nunn that we don't like showed up and we had to give him a glass of buttermilk and a biscuit with molasses hoping he would eat and leave. But no, he plunked down on a chair and set to with Grandpap. At first they were polite enough. Then Mr. Nunn kept on about people should be able to have slaves if they wanted, what right did some people have to say how others should live and that the Bible said Negroes were not the same as us.

Grandmother got red but she would never say anything. Grandpap made up for it. He told Mr. Nunn nobody had the right to own another living being. Mr. Nunn said for us to look out in the field. We owned our horses, didn't we? We owned the cows and pigs and the land, didn't we? Why couldn't we own slaves to work that land and take care of our horses and cows and pigs? I didn't hear much else as Grandmother and I retreated to the back porch to sort through the quilt box.

After Mr. Nunn left, Grandpap fussed about everything. The beans weren't done. Why hadn't Grandmother mended the screen door yet? Why was I bothering generals with letters about horses? He really fussed at me and Grandmother when we went to bring Dick in. He called him a good-for-nothing and said we should leave him out so passing soldiers could take him. Grandmother patted Dick's nose and told him not to listen to Grandpap. I did not talk to Grandpap the rest of the night. Until he made some popcorn and told me I was like Grandmother and told the little story of Grandmother getting lost at a horse race. Then I only spoke to him a little.

I want to go home. But Papa will not come to get me until day after tomorrow. If you were here and there were no war it would be the way it is supposed to be. Do you ever have popcorn? I think they should serve it when generals meet and maybe they would go to sleep like Grandpap and forget about the war. Maybe I will ask Grandpap to saddle Dick and take me home. Or maybe I will ride him bareback or maybe I will walk all the way home. Maybe I will take Grandmother with me.

Sallie

December 10, 1862

Dear Sallie,

That is some letter you wrote to the generals. Don't worry about not getting letters. You will. Everyone likes to brag about his horse. Grandpap has always had crotchety spells. You know he thinks being at war state against state is the worst thing that has happened to this country and that there should have been some way to avoid war or at least stop it quickly. He will be all right after this business is over. I am not looking forward to my birthday and Christmas away from home. The birthday pack-age arrived from Mama and Papa and you and Grandma. I still have some dried apple pie left. Yours and Grandma's cookie cakes were reduced to crumbs, but I ate every one. It is easy to see you are the writer in the family.

William

February 1863

Dear William,

We are anxious to hear from you. It has been so long. Did you get your Christmas packet? Papa is so worried that he frowns all the time and says almost nothing. Mama tries to talk to me and cheer me up but I catch her staring into the air and I know she is thinking of you. Every time we hear of another terrible battle we are afraid for you. A letter came today addressed to me and we were so glad thinking it was from you. But we didn't recognize the handwriting and that scared us for a bit until I said it must be an answer from one of the horse generals. It turned out to be a letter from General George Thomas. He told me about his big bay horse Billy. The first picture for Isaac to draw. That is, if you don't count Foster and Belle and Traveller. The Traveller picture is magnificent, the best Isaac has done. He doesn't have a picture to go by for Billy, but Papa and Mr. Mills said Gen. Thomas was a really heavy man and his horse would have to be big. Papa says Thomas is from the South and chose to fight for the Union and that the South hates him for that and the North distrusts him, so maybe since he doesn't have a lot of friends and likes horses is why he wrote. One thing he does not have is much imagination. I can think of a hundred names I would name a horse before calling one plain Billy. It was exciting receiving a letter like that, but I would give it up in a minute for one from you. Please write.

Love, Sallie

December 27, 1862

Miss Sarah Burd
Brewers Mill, Kentucky

Dear Miss Burd,

My apologies for the treatment your dog
received from those guerrillas. They do not
deserve to call themselves soldiers. No soldier under my command is allowed to whip
or rough handle any horse, or he will
answer personally to me. Mistreatment of
any other animal is also not tolerated.
Animals respect those who respect them. I
have a pack of dogs who station themselves by my tent each night hoping for a
small bit of food, which I always have
ready. At first they made my horse Billy
nervous, but he has gotten used to them.

Billy is a fine animal. He is named after

my friend General William T. Sherman. In exchange for his services he receives the best care I can provide. He is a fine bay, standing sixteen hands high.

General George H. Thomas

March 1863

Dear Sallie,

I did send you and Mama and Papa a letter as soon as I felt like writing, but if you haven't received it yet then it was lost as it was almost a month ago. That means you did not know I was wounded. That explains why you did not mention my injury in your last letter. I wondered. It was not a bad wound. A shot dug a hole in my outer thigh. Nothing serious on its own, but the spooky horse I had for the day lunged when I was hit and smashed my leg into a tree, crushing my leg between his side and the tree. Nothing broke, but the doctor said it was the worst bruise he had ever seen. My leg swelled out to a severe pone and ached so that I was sick to my stomach with the pain for several days. There was no way I could move to get comfort. They wanted to send me home to recover, but the idea of a thumping train ride with my leg throbbing was more than I could bear, even though I wished to see you all more than anything. So I stayed in the hospital until I could get around, then rejoined my company. My leg is healing but still sore. I limp around camp and sit down slowly and get up even slower. I had not been on a horse since it happened until three days ago.

I am not surprised General Thomas wrote you.

He likes horses as much as we do. You will get more letters, Sallie, wait and see.

Yesterday after your letter arrived I walked over to the horse corral to see if I could spot me a good calm mount. There was another soldier there and his back was to me and at first I didn't realize who it was. This soldier was favoring one of his legs too, and as we both appeared interested in a big roan we hobbled down the fence to have a better look. He turned to me and I saw that my companion was none other than U. S. Grant himself! He said a horse had fallen on his leg and asked me how I'd hurt mine. I told him a horse did me one better, that he ground my leg against a tree after I'd been shot. The general shook his head and made an *umpph* sound and then we stood by the corral and talked horses for a bit. Someone came and requested his leave before I had a chance to talk to him about you and your book. I guess that shows you that you never know who you might stand next to on any given day in the old state of Mississippi.

Tom is sick with a bad cough. Now that it has finally stopped raining every day maybe he will get better. He was mighty pleased that you heard from Thomas and says he will dance a jig if you hear from McClellan or Jeb Stuart. We have some wagers on the number of responses you will get. Rob claims you will be lucky to get one. I think you will get at least four or five. Tom has the most generous wager. He says thirteen for sure. How many letters have you mailed up to now? Will stop for now so I can send this on and you will quit worrying and know that I am still here and kicking, though not as much with one leg as I would like.

William

March 30, 1863

Dear William,

We are so glad you are better and your leg is healing. Mama said she knew something was wrong but she will tell you that in her letter, which by the way she is going will be a long one. I hope you get a better horse this next time around. Isaac said he read that almost all the horses ridden in battle at Seven Pines were killed, which might explain every horse's terror in battle.

I have now sent Grant a letter as well as Meade and one to a Mr. Douglas who knew General Ashby, who Mr. Heath says was a legend with his horse in Virginia. I am glad you and your friends are amusing yourselves with wagers on how many replies I will receive. Your friend Rob had better be wrong because I have already spent too much time writing out

letters to get only one response. I am like you.
I will be very pleased if I get five answers.
That way we would have at least seven horses
counting Foster and Belle. Tom thinks thirteen, does he? That means I will have to send
out a lot more letters or he won't have a
chance of winning.

Mama and I are making you a quilt. She will
tell you about it too. It is a nine patch and I
think one of the prettiest. Mrs. Newsome gave
us some wonderful material that is a deep red-
dish brown with little leaves printed on it. We
will quilt it different from most nine patches—
we are going to quilt stars in each big patch
and stars around the edge. I am dreading the
quilting part. We are still piecing now which is
tolerable, but I do not make stitches small
enough or straight enough to suit Mama.

Isaac finished the picture of Billy. He made
Billy look big and imposing which would please

Gen. Thomas. Get well and get a good horse this time.

Love, Sallie

April 1863

Dear William,

We have received our second letter. It is from General Thomas J. Jackson and it was a nice long letter from old Stonewall. I wonder if he knows everyone calls him that. Stonewall loves his horse. You can tell that by the way he writes about him. Little Sorrel must be as tough as Jackson or he couldn't keep up going up and down the mountains over there. Papa says Jackson's men march even at night to surprise the Union companies after them. Even though he does not support the Southern cause, Papa does seem to have great admiration for Jackson. He says if the South had more like Jackson the war would have been done and over or at least the North would be in trouble. What do you think of Stonewall? Do you hear much about the Confederate generals? Everyone here was surprised that Stonewall wrote us. They thought he would not be likely to bother. I think he has a little daughter at home and wrote me because I was a girl and it reminded him of her, or perhaps he wanted someone to know what he thought about his faithful horse. Anyway, Isaac is almost finished with his drawing of Little Sorrel. He had to do it twice because it was hard to get the color right. This is the third picture Isaac has done. Now we have a bay, a gray and a red horse.

Isaac and his family heard at last from Frederick. He has lost part of his right ear. At first his hearing was gone, but it is gradually coming back. We were all glad to know that he is recovering well.

It has rained a lot, but we finally got our garden in and Mama's plants we moved from her plant bed are looking strong and good. The mud came through to my socks and the orange mud stain will not wash out so I have permanent orange sock toes. Mama says she will have to make me some new dark ones so if I get mud on them it won't show. I refuse to wear ugly dark socks. Maybe it would be okay while I am at home but not going to town. Grandma's March flowers were thicker than usual this year, and because it rained and stayed cool so long they stayed in bloom longer. I hope there were some pretty flowers somewhere for you to let you know spring is here even if there is an ugly war going on. At least you will not be cold in camp anymore.

Love, Sallie

March 20, 1863

Dear Miss Burd,

You have asked about my horse Little
Sorrel. I almost did not choose Sorrel out
of that corral at Harpers Ferry, although
many think I deliberately took him to
bait them because he was the ugliest one
in the captured stock. At first I thought
Sorrel was too small, but although I can't
say the same about generals, there is with
certainty more to a good horse than
looks. A good horse has to be smart.
Sorrel never misses a thing. When I first
saw him, the other horses were nervously
pacing. Sorrel watched me while keeping
clear of the milling horses around him. A
good horse has to be sound and strong.
Sorrel never misses a step no matter
what the weather or the ground he is

covering. He is never lame. A good horse has to have a good gait. On occasion I have fallen asleep while riding, testimony to Sorrel's pace. A good horse is good company. When we pause in our marches, Sorrel lays himself down like a dog. I like to have an apple or two for him then, but supplies are hard to come by and many times he has had to make do with a corn-cob, which seems not to bother him at all. Some evenings I cannot sleep, and Sorrel and I take solitary rides. If I think out loud, he will never accidentally give away my plans for the morrow. You can always trust a good horse.

May God keep you and yours safe,
Thomas J. Jackson

May 1863

Dear Sallie,

By the time you get this you will by all accounts already have heard of the death of Stonewall Jackson at Chancellorsville. You may have one of the last letters he wrote before that campaign began. It is one letter I will really want to hold and read when I get home. Papa is right. He was some general.

We had our share of rain here also. Mud got in everything. Even the horses had a tough time going. I have not seen any flowers like Grandma's, but we did cross through the edge of a woods that was thick with purple violets. Remember the patch of them by our plum trees? Are they still there? I hope they are hardy because they got a good trampling when we traveled through.

Say hello to Isaac for me. I am enclosing this

with Mama and Papa's letter so I will say hello to them myself.

Your brother William

May 25, 1863

Dear William,

I will surely keep General Jackson's letter safe for you to see. I have mailed eight more letters now. I think that will be the last of them, as it took me every night last week to finish them. These were to Burnside, Joe Johnston, Sheridan, Morgan, Forrest, Ingalls, Pleasonton, and Taylor. I had copied two of them earlier but decided to mail all of them at once so I could easily remember when they were sent.

Since I will be twelve next month Mama is going to let me spend a whole week in town at Lucilla's. I am looking forward to the visit but would rather have a visit from a brother of

mine who is away sleeping in a tent and keeping safe I hope.

Grandmother is here today and we are going
over to the Mills after dinner. She wants to see
Isaac's drawings. We have been cleaning the
porch closet and the smokehouse all morning,
so I am ready for a break. Mama is calling me
for dinner so I will close. I am all written out
anyway after all those generals' letters.

Love, Sallie

June 8, 1863

Dear William,

I have spent the past week at Lucilla Tate's.
Barbara Newsome was there also. We had a
good time most of the time. We climbed out on
the roof one night which Mrs. Tate did not
appreciate, and we braided our hair every
which way and we tried on some of Mrs. Tate's

old dresses and petticoats and we went to the general store a lot because Nathan Hardesty was there working for his father and Lucilla is sweet on him, but Barbara and I think he is surly and not very nice. We also walked to the bluff and had a picnic and could see all of Benton from there. We made figures out of hickory nuts and pinecones, and I put a half walnut shell on the front of mine to make it look like it was playing the mandolin and gave it to Papa. We also sewed and stuffed and traded friendship pillows with our three names embroidered on them.

The last day we were there I talked them into going to the blacksmith stables to have a look at the horses. There was a beautiful bay stallion that I would like Belle to meet up with. He let us pet him, but the stableboy yelled to watch out, that he bit. He didn't of course—he just didn't want us bothering the horses. When we started walking back to Lucilla's she said her hand felt dirty and she held it up and smelled and said shoo it smells like an old horse. I smelled my hand and thought it smelled divine and suddenly wanted to go home and never come back to old Lucilla's again. I told her I loved the smell and was not going to wash my hand so I could smell it the rest of the afternoon. Lucilla flounced her skirts and said you would. That is one reason I will not be going back to Lucilla's soon.

The other is that when I got back home everything had changed. The big catalpa tree that was outside my window is gone. Papa said a limb broke off while I was in town and he thought the tree was old and too close to the house and chopped it down. There is nothing there but a stump. I cannot believe Papa did that. He could have at least waited until I was home and I at least could have watched him cut it, which must have taken him all day and Isaac and Mr. Mills were over to help. Or maybe if I had been home I could have talked him out of cutting it down. I cannot believe that he cut down my tree while I was gone.

And that is not all. While I was away for one week two letters came. The whole week they were here and I did not know it. Mama let Isaac read them so he could start work on the horse pictures so he has been working away and I did not even know we had heard from General Wade Hampton and that Mr. Douglas that I wrote to. Mr. Douglas wrote back about Ashby and his stallion. Isaac will have a grand time drawing that white stallion. This all goes to show, when you go away for just a bit everything changes on you. I promise you, William, I will keep everything I can the same for you here at home. I will not let them change a single thing more until you get home. Also Papa has found a stallion for Belle. I

have not seen him yet and I will hide Belle in my
room if I do not like the looks of him.

Sallie who no longer
has a tree by her window

P.S. I wish you would write to me again. Mama
and Papa let me read the parts to me you put in
their letters, but I would like my own letters
again from now on please.

April 3, 1863

Miss Burd,

You were most fortunate, Miss Burd,
to have your good mare set free to
return to you. Horses are vital to this
war effort, which makes some take
rogue methods to secure them. My
own Millwood plantation has fur-
nished horses for four cavalry companies. Many of the nation's finest
horses, as well as its finest men, will
be lost before this business is done.

But you asked about my own
mount. Butler is a powerful bay from
Millwood. We were trapped once by
Federals, penned against a fence,
fighting with swords. I had suffered a
cut or two when two of my men rode
up and intervened. Blinded by a

bleeding cut, I turned Butler toward
the fence and spurred him, hoping he
sensed the urgency of the moment. He
cleared the fence even as a piece of
shrapnel found my side. In the tur-
moil of the fighting a lesser horse
would have lost his rider.

Take care of your mare and foal.
There is little finer than watching a
long-legged foal grow to maturity. Do
not mourn your brother's loss of his
stallion overmuch. As with Butler, his
duty that day was to save his master.

Respectfully,

Wade Hampton

April 10, 1863

Dear Miss Burd,

Your letter regarding General Turner Ashby and his horse was delivered to me yesterday. It is a good thing you are doing, putting together accounts of horses of the war. Writing does help get us through hard times especially if we cannot control the day-to-day outcome of our world, as no one can when a war is being waged.

I do know how strongly General Ashby felt about his horse and believe he would have wanted me to write you about him.

Nowhere in either cavalry have I seen as magnificent a horse and rider as Ashby and his white stallion, Tom

Telegraph. It was as if they were drawn from legend, a knight and his steed. Tom could outrun anything, and Ashby loved to show up unexpectedly in front of a company of Yankees, daring them to chase him. On a day I shall always remember, I watched as a column of Union soldiers approached. It looked as if their leader were dressed in gray, which somewhat perplexed me. I was not puzzled for long, however. For as they drew closer I saw that the man on the white horse wasn't leading them; he was being pursued by them, and it was none other than Ashby and Tom. When they reached the bridge, the general pulled up to light a fuse his men had planted there but the Union soldiers closed

in and wounded Tom. The courageous stallion thundered across the
smoldering bridge, carrying Ashby
to safety before collapsing. General
Ashby bid him farewell with a last
stroke of Tom's mane. Sadly, not
long after, the general was lost to us
as well. There was never a greater
match in horse and rider than
General Turner Ashby and his white
stallion. They were a sight to see.

Sincerely,

Henry Kyd Douglas

June 1863

Sister Sallie,

Every time I sit to begin this letter I am interrupted. I do hope it arrives in time for your birthday. I am sending you a locket Tom found along the road. A horse must have nicked it walking by as it has a dent on the top. Still it is in good shape and the vines etched on the front look like they spell out an S to me. There was no picture in it and I do not have anything to put inside it, but I think you will like it.

Now that is something, to get two letters at once. We have all heard of Wade Hampton and some of us about the white horse of Ashby's. You have enough for a small book already. Did you see Lucilla's sister Anna when you were there? I remember her red hair under her bonnet, but she was always too shy to dance with anyone. A happy birthday to you back home.

With good wishes, William

July 30, 1863

Dear William,

I know Mama already sent you notice about Frederick's getting killed at Vicksburg. Such a terrible day. Mama and I were sitting in the shade shelling beans when we heard someone coming. It was Isaac. Only he wasn't carrying his drawing satchel or whistling or hurrying along the way he always does. He was walking along so slowly, his arms hanging at his sides as if they were heavy as blacksmith's anvils. He didn't even look at me. He walked right up to Mama and said Mrs. Burd, Frederick's been killed and Mama's in a bad way, I think you'd better come. Mama dropped the pan of beans and jumped up and grabbed Isaac and hugged him fierce and then she took off running across the yard, hollering I'm coming Hazel. She didn't even take her apron off or get her bonnet.

Isaac bent down and started picking up the beans. I just sat there like a stump. I couldn't move or say anything. And finally what I did say was so stupid. I said I was thinking of giving Belle a good currying. Isaac nodded and we walked to the field and caught Belle and tied her in the stables and we started brushing and currying, Isaac on one side and me on the other. We had not said a word the whole time. Peaceable came in and stood and watched us. Then Isaac stopped currying and put his head against Belle's shoulder and began to cry. I have never heard anyone cry so hard. He gasped and moaned and shook so, but Belle only laid her ears back and stood still and let Isaac cry against her. I didn't know what to do, so I rested my head on Belle's other shoulder. But I did not shed one tear. My face was hot and tight like a tick and I have never felt so bad for anyone before, but I could not cry.

That is how Papa found us, one on each side of Belle, our faces hidden against her gray speckled hide. Isaac followed Papa out of the stable. I untied Belle and slipped her halter off and kissed her nose. Where Isaac had laid his face there was a large round wet spot with streaks of tear tracks running down Belle's fat curved side. Papa and Isaac were sitting on the back steps. Isaac had his head on Papa's shoulder like a child. Papa told me to get a dipper of water and a cloth. He wet the cloth and wiped Isaac's face. Then Papa had me go into the kitchen and load up every good thing from the cupboard, even the pecan pie we had just baked for his birthday tomorrow with the last of the sugar that Mama had hoarded for two months. I wanted to cut at least a small piece to keep but Papa frowned when he saw me with the knife. I thought to myself, there will be nothing left for us to eat on Papa's birthday but turnip greens and bacon grease.

There was already a big crowd when we got to Isaac's place. His mother grabbed him and clung to him and wouldn't let him move from her chair. His aunts and uncles and cousins all showed up before dark so Mama told Mrs. Mills that we would be back in the morning. I didn't get to say anything to Isaac because his cousins all surrounded him. His aunt Becky said we should have something to eat, so Mama cut us a biscuit and slipped a thin slice of ham in for each of us and we went home. The cousins were busy gobbling in all the food, but Mama would allow us only a lone biscuit.

Mama went back early the next morning while Papa and I stayed home and took care of the chickens and the milking, although Daisy is drying up and there wasn't much milk. Mama came home at lunch and we celebrated Papa's birthday with corn bread and butter beans and weak tea without sugar and three fried chicken legs that Mama brought home from the Mills. Papa joked that he would like to see the chicken that three legs came from. Then just as Mama got the honey down for us to drizzle on our corn bread for dessert Isaac came up on the porch with a covered basket. We have so much and it is your birthday, Mr. Burd, Isaac said and he took the cloth off the basket and there were five pieces of pie and a piece of cake. And one of the pieces was Mama's birthday pie for Papa. Mama had tears in her eyes and Papa said it was the best birthday present ever. And Mama cut each one into four equal pieces and we each had a taste of every one. They were all good, but Mama's was the best. Isaac cleaned his plate too and said I think that was the first thing I've eaten since day before yesterday. Then he ate a wedge of corn bread and a small mess of butter beans.

I washed off the plate for Isaac to take home and found a rolled-up piece of paper in the basket. A birthday present, Isaac said. It was a drawing of Papa leading Bob and Roy. Papa was so pleased that he said he was going to make a frame for it right away and hang it up. Isaac asked if it would be all right for him to stay awhile and watch Papa make the frame since his mama was asleep and he needed a spell away from all of the cousins. Mama and I walked over to the Mills and I could see why Isaac needed to get away from the cousins.

August 5

Mama still goes over to check on Mrs. Mills every day, but she is doing better and is getting up and doing a few things. They heard that James is all right, which has cheered them up considerable. Isaac has not been over since

Papa's birthday. Papa says Gettysburg means the war will be over soon. I hope so.

Longing to hear from you, Sallie

August 1863

Dear William,

The most exciting thing has happened! We have heard from General Robert E. Lee. When he read Lee's letter Isaac smiled his old smile for the first time in weeks. Now for certain we can use his picture of Traveller in our book. We had decided we would include it even if Lee did not write, as the picture is too beautiful not to. Isaac says he knew Lee would write. We have had five responses. That makes seven horses in our book counting Belle and Foster. There are still fourteen letters unanswered.

Speaking of letters unanswered please write.

Sallie

June 2, 1863

Dear Miss Burd,

I have newly finished composing a
letter for my family of the day's
activities, and writing it put me in
the mind of your inquiry about
Traveller. I do have other horses I
ride, but my colt is the one I seek
most often. No matter how long the
day or the march, he never grows
tired or weary. He will remain with
me as long as we both breathe air on
this earth. I envy you your farm,
your good mare, and the improving
health of your dog. May your brother
return safely to you.

When I rest, I think of my family
and our farm. To remind me of
home, I have a small hen that stays

with me. Where she came from I no longer recall, but she is as loyal as my colt, delivering me a daily egg for my breakfast. You see, even in war small domestic connections keep me mindful of home and loved ones.

With sincerest best wishes,

R. E. Lee

August 30, 1863

Dear Sallie,

I have written both Isaac and Mr. and Mrs. Mills letters about Frederick. I wrote all the good times I remembered and how all us young fellows admired Frederick for his fine riding—nobody could outrace him—and the way he never spoke bad of anyone and never picked a fight or let anyone egg him into something he did not want to do. Of all people he should not have had to go to war. But I could not talk him out of it. Treat Isaac kindly as he was closest to Frederick.

Hearing from General Lee is a feather for you and Isaac. Keep working on the book. I do not know where the letters are from the Union camps. I know we have horses as fine as the Rebels. Do not worry overmuch about me. I want to think of you at home feeding the chickens and petting the new foal and spoiling Belle and sleeping safe in a bed without guns booming in the distance.

William

September 1863

Dear William,

Tell your friend Tom to cut a jig. We got a letter from J. E. B. Stuart. He sure thinks highly of himself and his horses. I can see him with his great plumed hat riding like lightning across the fields and around the Union soldiers. He is probably a lot like Ethan Gilliam who was always polishing his shoe toes on his trousers if he got a speck of dirt or spot of water on them. He was the only one in school with covers for his shoes when it rained. Isaac is in a quandary about which horse of Stuart's to draw. He thinks Virginia since Stuart escaped on her. I think "bold" Skylark. But as we don't have descriptions for either one, I suggested whichever we can find out about will have to be the one. Does Tom know about Stuart's horses?

We have finished today reading three newspapers

that Papa brought back from town. They are yellow and worn already because Mr. Heath had them at his paper for everyone to read in town for over a month. The war news is old but we read it anyway. It sounds bad. So many have died. I asked Mama yesterday if they would start taking women and girls to replace all the men who have died. She told me I didn't have to worry and she also told me some women do help out in hospitals. Have you seen any of these nurses? Papa said some women are spies, especially for the Confederacy. Have you heard of any of them? I am afraid so many horses have been lost that they will come looking for Belle and Peaceable and new little Dolly. We would not be so lucky this time I think. Don't forget to tell Tom to get dancing.

Love, Sallie

August 12, 1863

Dear Miss Sarah Burd,

I have had the greatest of fortune to be surrounded continually by the finest string of horses in our own or anyone else's cavalry. This is no small accident, as every time I see a fine high-stepping colt or beauty of a mare I mean to acquire them. My horses deserve to be set down in song and verse. Bold Skylark would travel to the ends of the earth if I asked him and get up tomorrow and return. Highfly outran the Yankees with me bareback and only a handful of mane to guide him. Ah, sweet Virginia, swift Virginia, my fabled mare that leaped easily a ditch full fifteen feet wide to take me out of the clutches of my enemy. Skylark, Highfly, Virginia, My Maryland, General, all of my animals eager to run wherever this Great Army wishes us, my remarkable, unstoppable flesh-and-blood descendants of Pegasus himself. Where my horses are, look for me. In addition to my fine horses, I too have dogs with me here. Nip and Tuck ride on the horses with me on occasion. Now there is a sight to see, old Stuart laughing with his dogs atop a stallion fit for a king.

Your Servant,
Major General
James Ewell Brown Stuart

October 13, 1863

Dear William,

Grandmother and Cousin Samuel and I have had a fish fry. We caught them in the creek while everyone else was at our hog killing. Papa wanted me to stay and help Mama, but Grandmother said I could come stay with her since Papa needed Grandpap to help more than Mama needed me and Grandmother. Grandpap and Papa think I need to toughen up. They say I will have to help kill hogs one day when I have a family of my own. But Mama said I could go to Grandmother's. Grandmother would not leave her farm while Grandpap was at our house because of the soldiers running raids.

Grandpap sent Samuel to guard us. He even gave him a rifle. Samuel is only a year older than me and Grandpap gave him a rifle. Grandmother took it away from Samuel as soon as Grandpap left. Samuel ran out to the pasture fence and pouted.

There has been frost here since last week but today the sun is warm. They may wish they had waited on hog day. It was a good day for fishing. At first Samuel would not go. He said Grandpap asked him to guard the house and we could not go to the creek. But Grandmother told him he could take the rifle so Samuel said he guessed we could go. I caught four bluegill, Grandmother caught five and Samuel caught seven. When he came home Grandpap was mad that we had gone to the creek. He said soldiers could have come by for water and found us. I notice that he was not so mad that it kept him from eating and smacking over the last three fish fillets.

Samuel is all right for a cousin. He thinks our horse book is a good idea. He thinks we should ask each general for a shoe from his horse and that we could put them across the mantel so everyone could see them. Grandmother said if you've seen one horseshoe you've seen them all so I guess I will not follow Samuel's advice. Maybe I should have asked for a hair from each horse. I promise to be happy with the letters. With all the rivers you are crossing and camping near I hope you can have a fish fry. They were so good. Much better than chitlings.

With love from your sister Sallie

October 28, 1863

Dear Sallie,

It is harder and harder for me to write letters home when we are so tired and worn. All I want is the war to end and me to come home. Everyone is so weary it is quiet most of the time at night with fewer songs or jests around the fires. Please know I wait for your letters and reread them again and again, so even if my writing has dried up like

Daisy write me as often as you can.

So many of my friends are gone. There is only Tom and me and a few others from our original company left. He did dance a jig when he heard you'd gotten a letter from Stuart. That was the only lighthearted thing I'd seen him do in a month and he always was a joker. We are both puzzled over Grant not writing. This will be quite a book and a shame that Grant will not be in it.

I think the war will be over soon. Am looking forward to seeing you all and Belle and Peaceable and Belle's new filly. My ear and throat have stopped hurting so much and I feel better and a mite cheerier than when I wrote the above. Now Tom has it and says the only thing that will make him feel better is when U.S. writes you. I told Tom not to hold his breath. I told some of the fellows about your fish fry and the next evening we managed to catch us a few creek fish and fried them up. Not much more than a taste apiece but good.

William

December 15, 1863

Dear William,

Mr. Heath has brought Isaac an early Christmas present. A fine set of oil paints with brushes. Now Isaac can paint the horses for our book. His drawings are good but to have color pictures would be nicer. Isaac is afraid he will not be able to learn to use the paints. He will I know it, especially now that he has General John Hunt Morgan's Black Bess to paint. She must have been a beauty. We both wish we could have seen her and wonder what happened to her. Note our last two letters have been from Confederate generals. Where is your General Grant's letter?

Mr. Heath brought Mama and me a bolt of fabric with blue and yellow flowers and a spool of blue ribbon. Mama is going to make new bonnets for us and there may be enough for a straight pinafore for me. Papa has helped me carve and polish wood flower holders for Mama and Mrs. Heath and Grandmother. I am sending you a surprise that I whittled myself. Mama and Papa have a package for you also. I wonder did you receive your birthday card from me? Isaac says sometimes soldiers get furloughed to visit their families. Do you have to ask for those? Or do you get picked? Every time I see someone walking down the road I hope it is you. Happy Christmas, William, wherever you are.

Your sister who misses you

November 1863

Dear Missy Burd,

The general would not approve me
writing this. But I saw it with my own
eyes. It happened right after we'd had
our last rest in Tennessee. That time
the pretty girls made such a fuss over
the general and took their sewing
shears to Black Bess so that General
Morgan had to post a guard and lock
the stable door to keep them from cutting off all Bess's mane and tail for
keepsakes. We left Tenn. and were
riding hard for Kentucky, but the
Union blue bellies crowded us to the
river. We had to leave all the horses
behind to jump the ferry. Bess didn't
take to being left behind, no, sir. She
shrieked and stomped and ran up and

down the bank, looking for a way to cross, mad at being deserted. The general never said a word, but I saw his wet eyes before he turned his back. I had to blink a time or two myself, knowing the prettiest little horse I'd ever seen would not again slip her muzzle into my pocket look- ing for an apple I'd hid. Whatever anyone thinks of the general, how hard they think he is, I saw his face when he lost Bess.

Your obedient servant,

Absalom Johnston

December 24, 1863

Dear Sallie,

Merry Christmas to you! I received your birth-day card and carry it in my pocket all the time. Also received the Christmas package and showed everyone the fine whistle you whittled for me with the merry bird's head on the end. If it had been a bigger gnarl of wood you could have made it into a horse's head like you said you tried to do. Your bird carving is just as good. I am also mighty grateful for the socks and underwear. I hope no one minds that I gave Tom the extra pair of socks.

Last night we had a pile of roast potatoes and Tom and some others in our company remem-bered a family less than a mile back whose house had been half shot and burned away and we got it into our heads to take them some of those abundant potatoes. We were feeling pretty good about ourselves until we got to the farm and the old grandma there said "thank you boys but potatoes is the one thing we got" and she opened a cellar cover and there was the prettiest pile of potatoes you ever saw. "Now if we just had a little meat besides skinny rabbit to go with those, now that would be a Christmas" that old lady said. So we dutifully rode back to camp and liberated a beef haunch and could have got shot, but McGruder owed Tom a favor and looked the other way.

So we are now back at camp and someone over the way is playing a fiddle and another a harmonica and we are all singing and our bellies are full and the weather is not unbearable and we feel practically civilized again having taken Christmas to that family. I think I will have one more of those hot potatoes before I turn in. The clouds just cleared above our tent and I saw a Christmas star or two before the clouds closed.

William

February 1864

Dear William,

We are glad you liked the socks and warm underwear we sent for Christmas. Mama cannot stand the thought of you being cold and not being inside at night when it is the dark of winter. I smuggled one of Fuzzy's kittens in last night intending it to sleep under the covers with me. But it went wild when I packed it inside and it scratched my neck and arm and Mama is afraid I will get cat scratch fever. The scratches are red and swollen but I do not feel bad. You would think a cat would want to come in where it is warm. Fuzzy used to sneak in to lie by the fire.

I had one little red itchy spot on my chin and Mama had to search me all over to make sure I did not have fleas from the cat. You know how she is about fleas. She did find one under my shirt on my back and took great triumph in squashing it between her fingernails. Isaac says James says he is covered in fleas and is thinking about naming them. If you have that many please do not tell Mama as she would never be able to rest thinking you were crawling with fleas. Hope you are warm and well and flea free. In case you have forgotten, walnut leaves in your bedding will help keep the fleas away.

With love from Sallie

March 1864

Dear Sallie,

Fleas we can live with. Do not mention lice, mites and chinches. Soon we will have chiggers and mosquitoes. On top of rashes from head to foot that never stop. We took a bath in the coldest creek that wasn't frozen I've ever been in day before yesterday. The sun was not as warm as it seemed before we were wet and we managed to use up most everybody's soap, but we all felt better afterward. Send more soap when you get a chance. Happy found some herb that he cooked in water and used as nice-smelling tonic for his skin. I tried a bit on my neck and face and it was refreshing. I recognize the smell but cannot call the name of the plant. Happy is a new man from up around Lexington. He is not disturbed by much and keeps us cheered up. After we cleaned up in the creek, we took our horses down and got them sudsed up too and wiped them down and walked them brisk until they steamed off the wet. They seemed to appreciate it. We could use a few more currycombs. Some fellows could use them on their beards.

William

April 1864

Dear William,

Daisy has calved. Twins. They are small but perfectly fine. Papa could not find her yesterday morning and we walked to the back of the woods to the little meadow she likes and she was not there either. We searched the woods and found her standing pitifully by the old creek bed. She was in some trouble so Papa had me run and get Mama and a rope. Mama had to hold Daisy's head with one rope and Papa had to reach inside to grab the calf's legs with the other. He got them but when he pulled he saw they were legs from two calves and pushed them back and felt and got two from one little calf and pulled her out and then Daisy managed to push the second one out. I thought Daisy would die from all that pushing and shoving. She was tired for a bit and Papa and Mama and I rubbed off the calves with Papa's shirt and

Mama's apron. Then Daisy came over and started licking them. She and the calves are fine. They were wobbly at first, but already today they are beginning to move surer. They both know where supper is. I have never seen two calves eat so much. They are both heifers and pale in color like Daisy.

Isaac is busy drawing McClellan's big bay. The general's letter was a good one but Mama already told you that in her last letter. At least that is one other Union horse to put in our book. I hope you don't mind too much that I am tacking my sentences onto Mama's letters sometimes. We are short on paper as we need it for our book and Isaac's pictures. Since you have the same scarcity and have been combining notes to me with Mama and Papa's I thought it would be all right. But I know separate letters are best so I will keep up as much as possible and hope you do the same.

Love, Sallie

16 Feb 1864

Miss Burd,

It would please me to have my horses
recorded in your journal of warhorses.
There were those on my staff who did
not appreciate Daniel Webster, but
they disliked him only because their
own mounts could not keep up with
Dan. I personally can attest I've never
had a finer horse. As to his size, he is
well over seventeen hands; in color he
is a dark bay; in conformation he is
unparalleled.

My other mount, Burns, had a bad
habit that may amuse you as it has
others, though of course they were
not in the saddle when it occurred.
Burns had a wild streak to him that
no matter how I worked with him

could not be corrected. This stub-
bornness manifested itself at dinner-
time. No matter where we were,
Burns bolted for the barn and oats. I
sidestepped this minor aggravation by
riding him only in the mornings, at
which time he was a perfectly good
mount.

Dutifully yours,
Geo. B. McClellan

April 1864

Dear Sallie,

I hope Grant's letter is on his way to you.
With his promotion to general-in-chief of the

Union and his move to Virginia, he may not have a chance to get back to you. He will make a good general to be in charge but we will miss him here. We will be with Sherman and from the looks of things traveling hard. We are laying in supplies, and horses and mules are coming in regularly. Sherman has some fine horses of his own. Sam the one he rides on long days is a big bay, part thoroughbred, and he sets a wicked pace I can tell you. The rest of us are ready to call it a day but Sam looks like he could go straight through till the morning. I cannot remember if you wrote General Sherman or not. He is a brusque fellow and in all probability would not bother to reply. But if you want to know more about Sam I will find out what I can. There's another fine thoroughbred the general has as well. He reminds me of Foster. We are preparing to move again. Am looking forward to your next letter.

Your brother William

May 3, 1864

Dear William,

You have a schoolteacher for a sister. At least I was one for almost all of one day. Miss Perry took sick last week so Mama taught school in her place. It was the last week anyway and not all of the children especially the older ones were there as they were busy on the farms. Isaac wasn't even there. But big Billy McKendree and his cousin Ed were there. Mama got a headache on Thursday, but instead of dismissing the school she called me outside and told me what lessons to do. I told her no I couldn't do it and she told me I could and that the children had come for school and to finish up and that I was a grown girl and I could take over a class of children for half a day. Then she went home.

It was the longest afternoon I have ever spent. The children laughed when I told them I was the teacher for the rest of the day. Big Billy said he didn't come to school to be bossed by no girl. I tried to get them to do sums and read some and they started throwing twigs and bits of leaves they must have had in their pockets. I finally had the idea to use the war in the lessons knowing I would get Billy and Ed's attention. We put the states where there had been battles on the big piece of slate and we were counting up numbers of men and boys we knew that had been in battles in each state when Billy said in a real low voice for everyone to be quiet. I was ready to be real mad at him when he motioned me to the window. There was a soldier at our well. He had a crutch and only one leg and he was so dusty and dirty that you couldn't tell what color his clothes were. He leaned against the side of the well and slowly pulled the bucket of water up. Billy said something about the man maybe having a gun and I was scared for a little but then the man looked up at us and nodded and began to drink water as if he hadn't had a drink in days.

I told everyone to get back in their seats, then I marched to my lunch pail and snatched it up and went outside. Billy never one to mind anyone went with me. When I offered the soldier my biscuit and sausage he reached out ever so slowly to take it as if it would disappear before he touched it. He took a bite and didn't even chew. Just held it in his mouth smiling and tasting, letting it melt on his tongue I reckon. After that first bite he ate the rest in quick chews and swallows. Then all ten of the other children including Billy and Ed were offering the soldier corn bread and bacon and blackberries and whatever else they had.

The soldier's name was Jeremiah and he was a Confederate and was heading home to Graves County. He told us he'd been traveling mostly at night because it was cooler and because he didn't want to meet up with anybody. I thought he meant other soldiers, but he said we were the first people he'd talked to in a week so I think he meant to avoid everyone. He seemed so tired. His voice even seemed tired and rusty. When he straightened up I expected him to creak like an old dried-up horse harness. He said he wished he could pay us for our food. We told him there was no need but he took out a slim book and held it out to me. He said he'd packed it all through the war and that it had saved his life once and that we should put it in our school. Then he walked over to the woods and out of sight. Billy said the dent in the book was where a shot had hit it. It was a book of poetry, so slim you wouldn't think it could stop any shot. It was inscribed to Jeremiah from your Molly April 1862.

After that we all shared what we had left for lunch and I took the bar of soap and washed out the bucket and dipper real well. Then I gave everyone a sum to do and they all did it even Billy and Ed. And we each read a passage to prepare for the last day's meeting. And it wasn't until everyone was gone that I realized that I had not had them do any spelling practice for the spelldown. Billy and Ed were waiting for me when I closed up the schoolhouse. They said there might be more soldiers around and walked me all the way to the curve where you can see our house. Mama was upset that a stranger came to the school and she wasn't there. But Papa said what could she have done that Billy and Ed and I couldn't. All of us may forget how to spell and cipher but we won't forget the day the one-legged soldier came to Enterprise school. I wonder if they will remember it was the day I was acting as teacher?

Your sister the schoolmarm

June 1864

Dear Sallie,

It is good news that Mama writes that at last you are recovering from your influenza. You were sick so long I began to really worry for you. I could not imagine home without you. Don't worry about the light hurting your eyes. I am sure that will go away and you will be as fine as ever. Mama says you are fussing to go outside. Tell her to let you sit outside. The fresh air will help make you feel better. I imagined the kerosene lamp and Mama reading to you and Papa plunking on his mandolin and Isaac describing the pictures as he was drawing them and me sitting there too, telling you of all the flowers and birds and squirrels and Belle and Charlie's latest antics. I was there with you as much as my thoughts could transport me. We have a lot of influenza, measles, dysentery, and everything else here. They are harder on us most of the time than shells. Mama says that James has suffered from influenza these past few weeks but is on the mend, which is good to hear. I would not like to lose another of my good friends.

Now that you are feeling stronger you can help Isaac put the book together. Mama also writes that you received a reply from General Meade's aide. With nine replies you have the makings of a fine collection even if you do not hear from any others. Congratulations on your success. I knew if they read your letter they would respond because you are such a good letter writer, how could they not. Tom is pleased as well although he will never forgive Grant his omission. Keep eating and getting stronger every day. Write when you feel up to it.

Your loving brother William

May 21, 1864

To Miss Sarah Burd,

General Meade requests that I
send you some facts about his charger
Baldy, which the General has owned
since shortly after First Bull Run,
where Baldy was wounded twice.
Baldy has carried the General to
Dranesville, Grovetown, South
Mountain, Antietam (where he was
again wounded and left for dead,
only to be found after the battle
calmly grazing, ignoring his neck
wound), Fredericksburg, Chancellorsville, and Gettysburg. At
Gettysburg Baldy was wounded in
the ribs and was pastured. The
General intends to take him home
with him after the war. Incidentally,

the name Baldy refers to his white
face, a distinctive marking for a dark
bay horse. The General knows of
only one other horse who suffered
more wounds as a battle horse.

Sincerely,

James C. Biddle

Staff Aide to Major General

George Meade

August 1864

Dear Sallie,

Last night the stars almost came down to camp
to join us. It was the darkest, quietest night we
have had in some time. I woke in the night to

hear locusts calling. I do not remember when I heard them last. It was a short respite. Before dawn the guns started, and we were packed and marching with the sun still below the sky.

I have a fine horse now. A bay mare. She is so good I almost do not want to ride her. She should be safe on a farm somewhere. Belle would be jealous of her, but Jenny is such a good girl she would win Belle over. She is no timid mare and lets the stallions know she is as good as them and they know to stay out of her reach if they don't want a swift kick or a good bite. When she is saddled, though, every muscle is waiting for my signal. She is not more than fourteen hands but very strong and stocky. She canters like a dream but when she breaks into a trot it is like riding across rocks. Still, I prefer her to all the others I've had, with the exception of Foster of course. And Belle. What does the book look like now? It cannot be too long until I see it for myself. I am glad you are getting stronger every day.

William

August 1864

Dear William,

I am almost completely well at last. I started another letter but never completed it so I am beginning a new one. I still get tired and lay down in the afternoon, but I am gathering eggs and picking in the garden and helping Mama although she keeps worrying I am doing too much.

Belle has a new foal. I don't know how to tell you about him. He is the ugliest thing I have ever seen. All knobby and big and his head is long and he does not look intelligent at all. He is plain brown all over, not a white marking any-where, and his mane and tail are exactly the same dull brown. What was Papa thinking when he brought that stallion over for Belle? Look what we got. Belle adores him of course and Peaceable and Dolly look at him the way I do, which is who is this ugly baby horse. Papa says he is part walker which is why he looks the way he does and he will grow into his looks. Mama feels sorry for him and calls him poor thing. He won't leave Belle's side and looks at us shyly from under Belle's neck where he hides. Belle can hardly graze for him getting in the way. Papa says we are getting too many horses and you need to come home and take care of them. He rides Peaceable sometimes and is training him for the cart. The Heaths want to buy Dolly. Papa is thinking it over. If they do take her she will be close by for you to see. We will keep Peaceable as he was Foster's colt. I do not think we will keep this ugly colt.

Papa has dragged some big corner rocks up from the creek for your blacksmith shop.

Sometimes in the afternoon we go and sit on them and plan for after the war. You should see the pictures Isaac has done. They are fit for a great palace somewhere. We are becoming quite famous for all our war letters and the pictures of our book. Even Mr. Mills who thought Isaac was spending too much time on it rather than his farm work said it was turning out good. My eyes still get tired when I read or write a lot or when I am out in the bright sun for a long time, but other than that I feel as good as new. What can we name this new colt?

Love, Sallie

October 1864

Dear William,

General Forrest has answered my letter. It was a short letter but in his own hand, and he did not tell us what King Philip looked like but Mr. Heath knew someone who had actually seen Forrest on K.P. and told Isaac what he looked like. Still no response from a certain Northern general.

We grew the most remarkable pumpkins and squash this year. They grew and twined around every post and tree they could reach. Last night we had a knock on our door just after dark and we opened the door and there was a figure with a pumpkin for a head. It was Isaac of course with a pumpkin balanced on his head and him peering out between the buttons of his father's big shirt. He drew a face on the pumpkin and put a hat on top. He brought us some wonderful muffins his mother had made and a jug of fresh cider and we set out on the porch and ate and drank while the moon came up. It was a nice night almost like summer with no frost. Owls called everywhere. Isaac left his painted pumpkin and we have it on our porch. Mama said that boy will draw on anything.

We are making pumpkin pies today. Mrs.

Newsome has not been well so we are taking a couple to her house. Wish we could get one to you.

Dolly likes it fine at the Heaths. They want to train her to pull their smart little buggy. It will be a pretty sight as she looks just like Belle, only taller and her mane is whiter. Please write.

Love, Sallie

September 11, 1864

My dear Miss Burd,

Twenty-nine. Someone started counting. Then we were all keeping track. I try not to dwell on it. Twenty-nine brave horses lost because I chose to ride them. I salute them all. Old King Philip, I hope they don't get him, but if they do, he'll go down with a mouthful of blue. He does hate those blue uniforms. Scares them, too, to have a big furious horse stretching his long yellow teeth for a bite out of them.

Not everybody's afraid of King. Why, down in Murfreesboro a kind lady asked me to back him up and then scooped a spoonful of dust from his hoofprint with her dainty silver spoon. That dust is by all accounts still on her mantel. Dust from old King's footprint. More than I'll have when this conflict's done. He deserves it, that old devil horse.

Your servant,
Lt. General Nathan B. Forrest

November 1864

Dear Sallie,

Forrest is some horseman. Every time we swap horse stories his name comes up and someone has a new tale. For a long time there if we heard a horse whinny in the night we sprang out of bed sure we were in for a raid from Forrest. He is like a demon rushing in and out with his men. There are more tales about him and Morgan. Some of them taller than the next. We did hear that Forrest's men sleep with their horses' reins wrapped around their arms so they can mount and ride at a moment's notice. And that if you see a fire in the woods or hear metal clanking it is Forrest getting his horses shod in the middle of the night with scraps they've collected and melted down. Be sure you keep that letter for me to read. I do not admire the man for much, but I do respect his horsemanship.

This next month has to be the last Christmastime away. And my one fervent hope is that my next birthday after this is spent with you all.

Love to all, William

January 10, 1865

Dear William,

We have received a letter from General Sheridan. It is about his great horse Rienzi which he now calls Winchester after the battle there. I understand him changing the name, but how will Rienzi know his new name? And Rienzi was such a beautiful name. If I ever have me a fine black horse I will name him Rienzi and nickname him Zi. This makes eleven replies. More than I ever hoped.

Isaac is struggling with the oils and brushes. He has trouble making the horses look round and real. He is using Belle as a model and finished one painting of her that looks passable, but he is not satisfied and is already painting over it. He wants more than anything to paint Rienzi and Traveller or Little Sorrel. His drawings are so fine and life-like, but the brush and paint are hard.

It is snowy here this morning. We had to break ice on the pond for Daisy and the horses but it is not so bitter cold now so maybe everything will thaw out.

There was terrible fighting at Nashville before Christmas. Everyone is saying the war has to end soon. I hope so. I want you to come home. I am also still hoping for a letter from your General Grant. I know he may not have two minutes where he can even sit and think his own thoughts much less write to a girl in Kentucky. You have not mentioned Tom in your last letters. Is he all right? I wish you and he were right here this minute.

Your sister Sallie who thinks of you always

December 27, 1864

Dear Miss Burd,

By now you have almost certainly
read about my faithful Rienzi and his
exploits of war. The reports are no
exaggeration. I have never owned a
more powerful horse. He is a big fellow at seventeen hands, black as coal
with white stockings and the deepest
chest of any horse I have ever seen.
He is out of Black Hawk Morgan
stock, I am told. Anything I ask of
my warhorse he does. He carried me
up Missionary Ridge and to victory
at Chattanooga, making him a hero
long before our ride to rally the
troops at Cedar Creek. I have taken
to calling him Winchester after our
victory ride, but do not be confused.

They are one and the same great horse. I apologize for my delay in answering your letter. Perhaps you no longer want to hear about the war or the horses.

Sincere good wishes in your endeavor,

Philip H. Sheridan

February 1865

Dear Sallie,

As you know from my letters to Mama and Papa we are on the move and traveling east. Everyone is tired including the horses. Those who have escaped being wounded are in fairly good shape but the marching is hard on them. Jenny picked up a rock and bruised her foot so I had to leave her behind and am now on a glass-eyed spotted gelding that is the only horse I ever wanted to spur to get going. He does not like to be hurried, but once we are all off he refuses to be left behind. I am looking for a dark horse with an easy gait. Old Spot makes too good a target. He was captured from some Rebels and climbs over rocks and hard places like a mule, but he will be replaced as soon as I can find another. We are getting to the heart of the war now. Do not be too angry with me for not writing more often and longer.

William

April 12, 1865

Dear William,

We have heard the news of General Lee's sur-
render to Grant. Papa says this is it, the war is
over, but Mr. Mills says there are other soldiers
who are still fighting. Were you anywhere near
the courthouse where Lee met Grant? Where are
you now? Can you come home? Just point your
horse's nose west and come home. I cannot wait
to see you again. I cannot believe that it is all
finally almost over. No more battles, no more
marches, no more soldiers roaming and stealing,
no more worry, no more you away from home.
Hurrah, hurrah! It is all about to end. Wait until
you see Belle and Peaceable. And the new side
porch. You will know me, won't you? You
won't think I am dull from not having been to
all the places you have seen? One thing I know
will please you is our book of horses. Isaac has

finished one fine oil. It will be a surprise when you see it. Oh, William, come home.

> *Waiting for you,*
> *Sallie*

April 24, 1865

Dear Sallie,

Papa's letter has arrived. It is only the third he has written me, satisfied to leave the writing to you and Mama and Grandmother. He said you were all upset badly by the President's death. It was the same here. To come this far and be so close to ending all this and have Lincoln gone in an instant. We wondered for a while if it would mean the war would somehow extend. But our generals will see to it that it is finished and we can get back to our lives once more. We cannot imagine Lincoln is not our leader any longer. Even those who were not solid behind him are saddened by his death.

When this is all over we will be a stronger country because he was here. We have all lived history this month. For four years we have. But we have lost so much. Please don't grieve so much, Sallie, that you lose April. It is still a fine month to be alive in.

William

April 30, 1865

Dear Sallie,

The long war is finally drawing to its end! I am sure you have all heard that Johnston has surrendered to Sherman, and this means me and the other boys will be coming home any day now. There are some skirmishes yet but we are not engaged. We are becoming quite jubilant here in camp and although we are waiting for the official word we all know the war is over. How I love to write that! Now if I only knew when I would be home. I was not at Appomattox but a friend of Tom's was and had a good look at Lee arriving on Traveller.

I hope you can recognize me when you see me. I have a beard and my face is so weathered I look like Uncle Tobe. Even if it had been a hundred years I would know all of you. Every night before I go to sleep the last thing I put in my mind is the farm and me walking the fields while the sun shines and the birds sing. I will have to turn in my horse and take a train home. He is a fine chestnut. I never did name him. I just call him Boy. So many fine horses gone. There could not have been a war without the horses. Tom wants me to bring Peaceable to Tennessee where he is going to live with his uncle as soon as he gets a couple of mares and he will have some descendants of Foster. I will write Mama and Papa as soon as I know for certain when I will be coming home.

William

Dear William,

I don't understand why you cannot come home yet! The war is over! Mama says she is going to make me stay in the stables with the horses if I do not calm myself. She never stops humming and singing from breakfast until bedtime. And Papa smiles at everyone including Charlie and Moll's new kittens which he never had time for before. Even Grandpap seems happy. He walks livelier and does not pick arguments as much. Grandmother is canning berries so you will have as many of your favorite blackberry cobblers as you want. Isaac is painting another portrait, the last one for the book. It does take the oils a long time to dry so it may not go into the book even by the time you are home. I cannot think of anything else to say except come home.

Love, Sallie

June 2, 1865

Dear Sallie,

Some of the boys have mustered out. But our company is still here. We have plenty to eat and are living less and less like soldiers at war. Some sutlers have come by and I have bought you and Mama a few pieces. I have a songbook for Grandmother. Tom and I are anxious to go home but we are skittish as wild horses about what to expect. Do not expect the William you last saw. I would recognize you in a barrel covered with straw. I will let Mama and Papa know as soon as I know anything.

Home soon.
William

June 1865

Dear William,

Papa and I had a busy day yesterday. Mama is

in town for three days setting type for Mr. Heath while Mrs. Heath goes to Bardstown to visit her family there. Mama makes money doing it, but I miss her and she says this is the last time she is doing it in the summer because she has too much to do at home. But whenever Winnie Heath comes and begs her to take over for her Mama always does. Anyway, Papa and I decided to clean out the stable as we were so busy planting that we hadn't got to do it proper yet. My two work dresses are so small on me now that I tore one right up the back, so Papa suggested I wear a pair of his trousers and his shirt and an old pair of your shoes. I tied my hair up with an old rag ribbon, and what a sight I was.

Papa and I worked hard and we were as grimy and sweaty as we could get when we heard someone halloooing from the yard. It was Greenberry Ford riding Mr. Ford's fine dapple gelding. He tried not to laugh at me but he couldn't keep his big white teeth from breaking through his dark lips. I told him he'd better not tell Tick about me dressed like this, and he sobered right up and said Tick had gone off to Paducah to be with his aunt Cilly. Then Greenberry told us that old Mr. Ford had up and given them all freedom papers and that Tick had picked up the next day and gone, but that he and Lucy were staying on with Mr. Ford for just a bit if nobody objected. I couldn't believe Tick was gone. He'd always showed me all the horses in the Ford stables whenever I'd gone there with Papa and I'd visited with him and Lucy and Greenberry in their little house under the big oak tree.

Greenberry came for any extra strawberries we had, because old Mr. Ford had come into a pile of sugar and had Lucy making up scads of strawberry preserves in the big house kitchen. Greenberry said we could have two jars of preserves for every handy of berries. Papa let Greenberry pick all but one row of our berries and put them in a flour sack that he had a carrier on his back to hold. Papa thought he was saving Mama some canning time and besides we didn't have that much sugar. I kept thinking of Lucy canning all those berries in the heat just because Mr. Ford wanted her to. I wondered how many jars she got to keep.

I told Papa I was mad at Tick going away and he said he wouldn't be surprised at Greenberry and Lucy picking up and going too now that they had their freedom papers. He said freed slaves were supposed to move out of state, but with the war and emancipation down the road folks might look the other way if old Greenberry and Lucy stayed to work for Mr. Ford. I can see him letting them stay in their cabin but I don't know if he would pay them anything, although Greenberry has always hired out. Still, I know when he came to help us with anything, whatever Papa paid him he turned over to Mr. Ford, and if Papa wanted Greenberry to have something of his own he had to slip it to him as something for his pocket. I cannot imagine them gone too. Although perhaps then Lucy could have her own church. I know there are Negro churches around Paducah.

Remember that spring she started coming to church and sitting on an old straightback chair under the pear tree outside the church? And when the organ would start, and the singing, she would sing too in that wonderful deep voice. And the third Sunday she did this Brother Grady walked out and asked her to come in and sing. She did that for three more Sundays. Sat outside and waited to be invited in.

Then on the fourth Sunday she brought Tick and Greenberry all dressed up in white shirts, but Brother Grady never came out that day even though we could hear Lucy singing her heart out. I remember whispering to Mama asking why didn't Brother Grady let her come in again? Mama shushed me. When church was over they were gone but the three chairs they'd sat in were still there. I watched those chairs for a long time hoping they'd come back. But they never did. When I asked Lucy why she quit singing she said she'd lost her voice. I know she didn't because I heard her singing one evening when we dropped off Elsie Ford after a dance in town. I asked Mama about it again, and she told me several people didn't like that Brother Grady had invited Lucy in and he knew it would cause a ruckus if three Negroes started attending. Tick and Greenberry and Lucy are the only slaves I have ever known. I don't want them to leave. But it would be something for Lucy to sing down the rafters in church again. That is the news from here.

Every day we look for a letter from you telling us when you will be home. We see someone walking down the road and hope it is you surprising us but it is always someone else. At least we know you are not in battles and are safe. But we want you home again. Forever and ever. I can't wait to walk the fields with you again and to help you set up the blacksmith shop and work and ride the horses. This is the hardest thing, waiting for your return.

Love, Sallie

June 1865

Dear Sallie,

Yes, I remember Lucy singing at the church. Even if you had not written me about her I would have thought of her this week as we passed a group of freed slaves traveling north with everything they owned strapped to their backs. Many of them limped from sore feet and they were as dusty as your school soldier, but as they passed one of them began to sing and soon all of them were singing as strong and deep as Lucy did. I hope there is a home and a church for them somewhere.

I have a bit of bad news. I had kept your letters in my knapsack thinking you might like to put them in your book too. Unfortunately two days ago we had a heavy rain and wind and our tent blew over and in the mess to right everything your letters got wet and several of them were ruined. I salvaged most of them and will bring them to you. To think that I carried them with me all of this time and here at the end have managed to lose some of them. There were six letters ruined. I should have taken better care of them or sent the parcel of them home for safekeeping, but I liked rereading them in the evenings.

We have had meals of good beef the last two days and Tom and I are feeling positively fat and lazy. We will be home by the end of the summer. I have written Mama and Papa all the details I know. We are keeping ourselves occupied with cards and sharing plans for when we get home. It is a different army now that the war is over. We are loud and boisterous one minute and quiet and reflective the next and off and on all day, and even waking at night we are restless and bored, ready to come home. Except for the few who want to stay in the army which are not me or Tom or any of our friends. We just want to go home. Don't curry off all Belle and Peaceable's hair getting them groomed to show off to me. What did you think of the blacksmith shop plans I wrote to Papa about? We would be sure to have plenty of horses around all the time if we had the smithy. Will be seeing you soon.

William

August 25, 1865

Dear William,

I cannot wait to see you at the station. It will be wonderful to have you home. We are busy getting ready. Mama wanted your quilt finished by the time you come home so we have been working on it every afternoon. Papa even threaded up a needle to help out. He is not bad but he keeps pricking his finger and we have no thimble big enough so he made him one of leather but he said it was too clumsy. Yesterday Mr. and Mrs. Mills and Isaac came over and threaded up needles and set to work with us so we could get it finished by the time you arrived. It was a funny sight, all those men quilting. The women in Mama's quilting circle sent word that they couldn't make it to help finish it. Miss Houser and Mrs. Watkins have the flu which is going around and makes you weak for days and days and Mrs. Canup had to go to Sledd Creek to take care of her daughter who has two new baby boys and Gloriana Harvey's right hand is swollen with arthritis until she can hardly do her daily chores much less quilt. We are so happy that you and James are coming home and that the war is over that we'd quilt by moon-light. The Mills still have not heard for sure when or where James will arrive.

Speaking of moonlight, the other night when the moon was full our mockingbird sang all night. He was fooled, I guess. I did not care. I was awake anyway because finally that day I received an answer from none other than Ulysses Grant himself. You were right, he sure does like horses. I would like to meet him. He talked of so many horses Isaac cannot make up his mind which one to draw.

I have named Belle's colt. It begins with a U, can you guess what it is? Isaac raised his eyebrows when I told him but he didn't say anything. Papa says some of our Rebel neighbors may not like it but I told him we would call him Uly. Papa said why not Buck and I said that was a dog's name. Ulysses has gone so long without a name that he may never learn one anyway.

Isaac and I are working to get our book finished. Mama has made a carrying bag for it like the quilt. Papa cut two straps of leather for it. I will bring it when we ride to get you. The book is beautiful because of Isaac's drawings. They even put it in the window of the paper for a week for everyone to see. Mama came up with a really clever way to put the letters on heavier paper. I will put our letters in it when you get home, as you suggested, although it will seem strange for others to read them. Isaac is coming with us and we will be driving Bob and Roy since Belle could not pull us all and Uly isn't trained to the wagon yet and Peaceable is too big to hitch with any horse around.

I hope you recognize me. I am taller than Mama now and my hair is darker with only a few fair strands left on each side. Isaac is as tall as me and is trying to grow a mustache. It looks like the sparse hair on a horse's chin to me but I haven't said anything. I am glad Tom is going safely home also. We all smile all day long knowing soon you will be back where you belong.

With love, Sallie

July 6, 1865

Dear Miss Burd,

I sympathize with you in your admiration of a good horse. Fortunate for you that your gray mare was set free to find her way home. I have been breaking horses since I was younger than you, being only ten years of age when they brought me horses to break. One of my proudest moments at West Point was the time I rode York, the wildest horse in the stables there. I am always looking for good mounts. Fox, my good roan, was with me at Shiloh. Kangaroo carried me at Vicksburg. I acquired him at Shiloh, a starved big-boned outcast until we brought him back to good health. Jeff Davis is a black pony with the smoothest gait I've ever seen. I intend to take him home with me. His gentle nature will make him quite suitable for the family. I have not mentioned Jack yet. To see Jack is to see an artist's creation of a horse. Cream-colored, dark legs and eyes, white mane and tail. When we have a parade or official review, I ride Jack.

The best horse I have had the privilege to own is Cincinnati. Everyone else seems to admire him as well. One gentleman offered me ten thousand dollars for him. He is the son of Lexington, the fastest four-miler in the country, which explains that monumental offer. No one rides Cincinnati save for myself, except on one or two occasions when I was generous and wise enough to let the President ride when he paid a call. One of the lesser-known traits of our fallen President was his keen eye for horses.

Your servant,

U. S. Grant

July 30, 1866

Dear Tom,

William will be traveling down to see you in less than a month to meet your bride and to buy that mare from your cousin, but I could not wait so am writing you to let you know that you were absolutely right. We had thirteen answers on warhorses, the number you chose. The letter from Grant gave us twelve, and after that I received a letter from a soldier who wanted me to put his horse Mack in the book. We thought you should receive a prize for your accuracy, so Isaac drew you a picture of Rienzi that is even better than the one in our book. We will send it by William. He does not want to bring the book itself because he is afraid he will damage it on the trip.

The day William came home last year was wonderful. It seems almost like a dream. On the same train with William was Isaac's brother James, which we did not expect at all. Such laughing and hugging and nobody cared that they fought on different sides. William and James were both thinner than I remembered, but they looked so much better than some of the other soldiers that we felt they were fine and healthy after all. William sat right down at the station and admired our book. But everyone was so anxious to get them home that I told him it could wait until later. So he closed it up and we practically galloped Bob and Roy home. It was a rough ride but nobody seemed to mind.

We were almost home when we heard a wild whinnying. Then through the bushes we saw Belle running up and down the fence. William made Papa stop the wagon and climbed over the fence and Belle snorted and bucked in her excitement like a stallion. Peaceable and Uly did not know what had come over their mother. William was some pleased, I can tell you, that Belle had not forgotten him. Neither had Charlie. He met us in the middle of the road barking and wagging his tail. It was the first time we had heard his voice since the soldiers came long ago. What a celebration we had that night. I ate so much I thought I might be sick, but William ate twice as much as me. We are having a social at church next Sunday to welcome everyone back and to say a prayer for those who did not come home.

Perhaps one of these days you can come and visit us here and we will sit in the shade and we will laugh and talk and be happy together as friends.

Your Friend Sallie Burd

June 1, 1866

Dear Miss Sallie Burd,

I have heard from a friend of mine about your letters requesting information and stories about warhorses. I thought you might like to hear about a horse who did not belong to a general, a horse that means more to me than any animal I have ever encountered. It was not long after Petersburg that we captured some Union horses. I picked out a stocky Morgan that someone said was from Maine. Twice between Cedar Creek and Appomattox I lost Mack, but luckily for me and my family he was returned to me both times.

At the end of the war I had suffered a severe throat wound and could not talk. Mack carried me home in that state. There was not much left of our home. We had to start over. We had only Mack to help us. That stout fellow pulled wagons loaded with stone, axes and tools. He pulled the plow over our forty acres and cut hay with a heavy mowing machine. I had a little land, less money, my own energy, and one fine horse to begin life again after the war. Without Mack and his great heart I couldn't have done it. When the mustered-out Union soldiers in town made fun of the puny Rebel horse reduced to pulling farm wagons, I longed to argue back but there was no point. Let them be blind to the courage of the best horse I will ever know.

Sincerely,
Edward McDonald
Cool Spring, Virginia

September 20, 1866

Dear Isaac,

I am glad that you are enjoying your visit at your cousins. The little mare you are bringing home sounds like a beauty. Some sad news here. Not more than a week and a half after William returned home from visiting Tom in Tennessee we received a letter from his uncle that Tom had died from typhoid that he contracted on a visit to Nashville. He had not been in the best of health since his return from the war and could not withstand the fever. His wife, Florence, was very sick but is getting better. She had Mr. Hiett—this is Tom's uncle—return my letter to Tom to add to our book. She requested to keep your picture of Rienzi.

Tom was planning to visit us this fall and I do regret so much that I never got to meet him. I regret almost as much that Tom never got to see the book he heard so much about. He believed with us that the horses who served in the war should not be forgotten. And by telling their stories, our stories small though they are were told as well. William has not said much in the days since he heard about Tom.

It is clouding up in the west like rain. Perhaps a good rain would make us all feel better. I am going now to see if William would like to take a ride down to the creek. It would give the horses a chance to get away from the horseflies that are plaguing them. Tomorrow Mr. Ford is bringing his horses over to have William shoe them, so it will be busy. William was asking last week if you would draw him a picture of his new stallion.

Your friend, Sallie

$\mathcal{E}$ach day in Lexington, Virginia, visitors leave apples, carrots, and scattered coins on the small flat nameplates marking the graves of two of the greatest warhorses of the Civil War. I like to think the tributes are not just for Traveller and Little Sorrel but for all the horses that galloped with them into history.

                                                      ~◌~